How to Catch a Star

Oliver Jeffers

Philomel Books

Once there was a boy

and the boy loved stars very much.

Every night the boy watched
the stars from his window

and wished he had one of his very own.

He dreamed of how this star
would be his friend.

They would play hide-and-go-seek

and take long walks together.

The boy decided he would try to catch one.
He thought that getting up early
in the morning would be best,

because then the star would be tired
from being up in the sky all night.

The next day he set out at sunrise.

But he could not see a star anywhere.
So he sat down and waited for one to appear.

He waited . . .

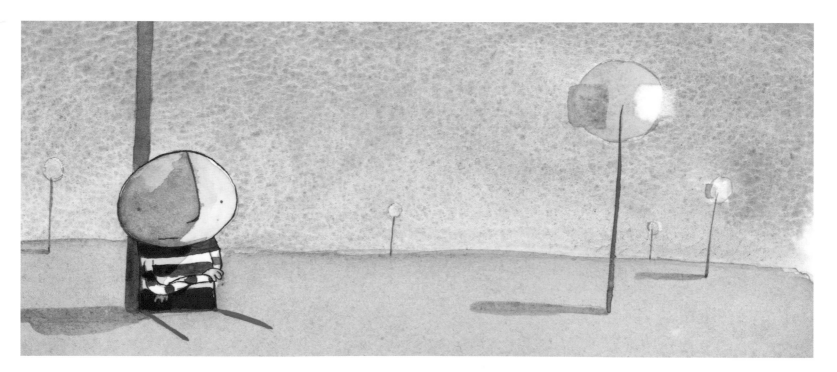

and he waited . . .

and ate lunch . . .

. . . and waited.

And after
dinner

he waited some more.

Finally, just before
the sun was about
to go away, he saw a star.

The boy tried
to jump up and grab it.

But he could not
jump high enough.

So, very carefully,
    he climbed to the top
        of the tallest
            tree he could find.

But the star was still way out of reach.

He thought he might
lasso the star with
the life preserver
from his
father's
boat.

But it was much too heavy
for him to carry.

If only he could fly up in a spaceship and just grab the star . . . but the only spaceship he owned was made of paper, and it didn't fly well at all.

Perhaps he could get a seagull to help
him fly up into the sky to reach his star?

But the only seagull he could find
didn't want to help.

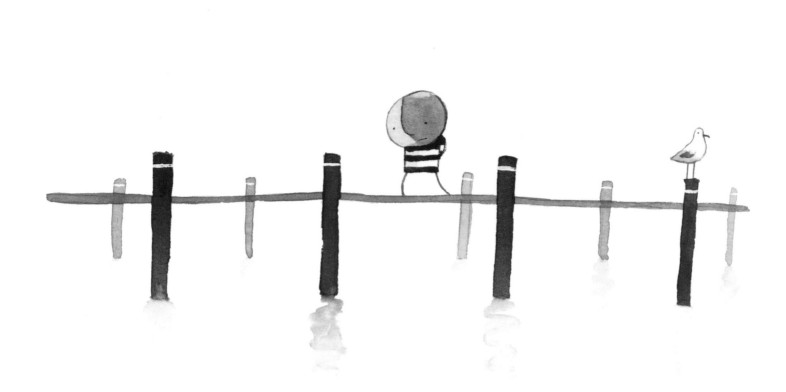

The boy worried he would
never catch a star.

Just then he noticed something floating in the water.
It was the prettiest star he had ever seen!
Just a baby star. It must have fallen from the sky.

He tried to fish it out with his hands.

But when the boy reached out to touch the star, it just rippled through his fingers.

Now the boy was sad. But in his heart,
the wish just wouldn't give up.

Slowly, he began walking home.

And that's when he saw it . . .

washed up on the bright golden sand.

The boy had caught a star!

For Marie and Paul

First American Edition published in 2004 by Philomel Books, a division of Penguin Young Readers Group,

345 Hudson Street, New York, NY 10014. Philomel Books, Reg. U.S. Pat. & Tm. Off.

Published in Great Britain by HarperCollins Publishers Ltd., London.

Manufactured in China.

Library of Congress Cataloging-in-Publication Data   Jeffers, Oliver.

How to catch a star / Oliver Jeffers.—1st American ed.   p. cm.

Summary: Eager to have a star of his own, a boy devises imaginative ways of catching one.

[1. Stars—Fiction.] I. Title.

PZ7.J3643 Ho 2004   [E]—dc22   2003020465

ISBN 978-1-9848-1358-9

Ages 3 and up

10 9 8 7 6 5 4 3 2 1

This special edition was printed for Kohl's Department Stores, Inc.
(for distribution on behalf of Kohl's Cares, LLC, its wholly owned subsidiary),
by Penguin Random House LLC, New York

Kohl's
Style: 42861
Factory: 123386
Production date: 10/2018

A star of his very own.